MR. BUSY

by Roger Hargreaves

© Roger Hargreaves 1978

Published by Thurman Publishing Limited
The Mill Trading Estate Acton Lane London NW10

There has never been anybody quite like Mr Busy.

He could do things ten times as fast as ever you or I could.

For instance, if he was reading this book, he'd have finished it by now.

He lived in a very busy-looking house which he'd built himself.

As you can see.

It had lots of doors and windows, and do you know what it was called?

Weekend Cottage!

Do you know why?

Because that's how long it took him to build it!

One fine Summer morning Mr Busy was up and about bright and early at 6 o'clock.

He jumped out of bed and had a bath and cleaned his teeth and cooked his breakfast and ate his breakfast and read the paper and washed up and made his bed and cleaned the house from top to bottom.

By which time it was 7 o'clock.

Busy Mr Busy!

Now, next door to Mr Busy lived someone who wasn't quite such a busy person.

In fact, a very unbusy person.

Mr Slow!

If he was reading this book he'd . . . . read . . . .
it . . . . like . . . . this!

He'd still be on the first page!

And that same fine Summer morning, at five past
seven, when Mr Busy knocked at his door Mr Slow
was fast asleep in bed.

He'd gone to bed for an afternoon nap the day
before and somehow hadn't woken up until he
heard Mr Busy knocking at his door.

"Who's .... that .... knocking .... at .... my ....
door?" he called downstairs.

"Good morning" cried Mr Busy "Can I come in?"

And, without waiting for an answer, he went inside.

"Where are you?" he called.

"Up .... stairs" came the slow reply.

So Mr Busy went upstairs, two at a time.

"Good heavens" he said "You're still in bed!"

And he made Mr Slow get up.

And he made his bed for him, and cooked his breakfast for him, and cleaned his house for him.

Poor Mr Slow.

He hated to be rushed and fussed.

"Right" said Mr Busy briskly "It's a fine day. Let's go for a picnic."

Mr Slow pulled a face.

"I .... don't .... like .... picnics" he complained.

"Nonsense" replied Mr Busy and busied himself around Mr Slow's kitchen making up a picnic for the two of them.

It took him a minute and a half.

"Right" he cried" when he'd finished "Off we go!"

And he bustled Mr Slow out of his front door and off they set.

As you can imagine Mr Busy walks extremely quickly.

And, as you can imagine, Mr Slow doesn't.

So, by the time Mr Busy had walked a mile do you know how far Mr Slow had walked?

To his own garden gate!

Mr Busy hurried back.

"Come on" he cried impatiently "Hurry up!"

"Hurry . . . . up" replied Mr Slow
"Im . . . . poss . . . . i . . . . ble!"

"Oh alright" said Mr Busy "We'll have a picnic in your garden."

"Wait a minute though" he added "The grass needs cutting."

And he rushed back to Weekend Cottage and rushed back again with his lawnmower and rushed up and down cutting Mr Slow's lawn.

It took him two and a half minutes!

It would have taken him two minutes but he had to mow around Mr Slow who couldn't get out of the way in time.

"Right" cried Mr Busy "Picnic time!"

And together on that fine Summer day they had a fine picnic.

Well, actually, Mr Busy had a finer picnic than Mr Slow because he ate more quickly and had most of the food.

Mr Busy stretched out on the grass.

"That was fun" he said "I like picnics!"

"You .... do! .... I .... don't" said Mr Slow.

"Tell you what" went on Mr Busy, ignoring him "Tomorrow we'll go on a proper picnic , out in the country."

Mr Slow pulled a face.

"And" went on Mr Busy "In order to do that and get you out into the country I'll have to call for you earlier than I did this morning."

Mr Slow pulled another face.

"See you tomorrow then" said Mr Busy, and went home and cleaned his house from bottom to top.

The following morning Mr Busy jumped out of bed at 5 o'clock and had a bath and cleaned his teeth and cooked his breakfast and ate his breakfast and read the paper and washed up and made his bed and cleaned the house from top to bottom.

By which time it was 6 o'clock.

He went and knocked on Mr Slow's front door.

"Come on! Come on!" he cried "Time to be up and about! Picnic day!"

No reply.

"Come on" cried Mr Busy again.

No reply.

Mr Busy went inside.

And went upstairs, three at a time, and into
Mr Slow's bedroom expecting to find him in bed.

But he wasn't.

And he wasn't anywhere upstairs.

And he wasn't anywhere downstairs.

"Bother" said Mr Busy "I wonder where he's got to?"

Where Mr Slow had got to was under his bed.

Hiding!

He didn't want to go on any picnic.

Not he.

"Bother" said Mr Busy again "That means I'll have to go on a picnic on my own!"

Under his bed Mr Slow smiled a slow smile.

"What .... a .... good .... idea" he said.

And went to sleep.

Snoring very slowly.